TIGERS FOREVER

Chapter 1

On the left bank of the river
Ganges, where it flows out from
the Himalayan foothills, is a
long stretch of forest. At one time
this forest provided a home for
some thirty to forty tigers, but men
in search of skins and trophies
had shot them all, and now there
was only one old tiger left.

Although the tiger had passed the

prime of his life, he had lost none of his majesty. His muscles rippled beneath the golden yellow of his coat, and he walked through the long grass with the confidence of one who knew that he was still a king, although his subjects were fewer. His great head pushed through the foliage, and it was only his tail, swinging high, that sometimes showed above the sea of grass.

One day, the tiger headed for the water of a large marsh, where he sometimes went to drink or cool off. The marsh was usually deserted except when buffaloes from the nearby village were brought there to

bathe or wallow in the muddy water.

The tiger waited in the shelter of a rock, his ears pricked for any unfamiliar sound. Then he walked into the water and drank slowly.

Suddenly the tiger raised his head and listened, one paw suspended in the air. A strange sound had come to him on the breeze, so he moved swiftly into the shelter of the tall grass that bordered the marsh, and climbed a hillock until he reached his favourite rock. This rock was big enough to hide him and to give him shade.

The sound he had heard was only a flute, sounding thin and reedy in the forest. It was played by

Nandu, a slim brown boy on
a buffalo, leading a herd of seven
others. Chottu, a slightly smaller
boy, rode at the back.

The tiger had often seen them at
the marsh, and he was not bothered
by their presence. He knew the village
folk would leave him alone as long
as he did not attack their buffaloes.
And as long as there were deer
in the forest, he would not need to.

He decided to move on and find a cool shady place on the hillock in the heart of the forest, where he could rest during the hot afternoon and be free of the flies and mosquitoes that swarmed around the marsh. At night he would hunt.

With a lazy grunt that was half a roar, "A-oonh!" – he got off his haunches and sauntered off. The gentlest of tigers' roars can be heard a kilometre away, and the boys looked up immediately.

"There he goes!" said Nandu, taking the flute from his lips and pointing with it towards the hillock. "Did you see him?"

"I saw his tail, just before he

disappeared. He's a big tiger!"

"Don't call him tiger. Call him Uncle."

"Why?" asked Chottu.

"Because it's unlucky to call a tiger a tiger. My father told me so. But if you meet a tiger, and call him Uncle, he will leave you alone."

"I see," said Chottu. "You have to make him a relative. I'll try and remember that."

The buffaloes were now well into the marsh, and some of them were lying down in the mud. Buffaloes love soft wet mud and will wallow in it for hours. Nandu and Chottu were not so fond of the mud, so they went swimming in deeper water. Later, they rested in the shade of an old silk-cotton tree. It was evening, and the twilight fading fast, when the buffalo herd finally made its way homeward.

Chapter 2

At dawn next day Chottu was in the forest on his own, gathering Mahua flowers, to be made into jam. Bears like Mahua flowers too, and will eat them straight off the tree.

Chottu climbed a large Mahua tree and began breaking off the white flowers and throwing them to the ground. He had been in the tree for about five minutes when he

13

heard the sound made by a bear –
a sort of whining grumble – and
presently a young bear ambled into
the clearing beneath the tree.

It was a small bear, little more
than a cub, and Chottu was not
frightened. But he knew the mother
bear might be close by, so he
decided to take no chances and sat
very still, waiting to see what the
bear would do. He hoped it
wouldn't choose the same tree for
a breakfast of Mahua flowers.

At first the young bear put his
nose to the ground and sniffed his
way along until he came to a large
ant-hill. Here he began huffing and
puffing, making the dust from the

ant-hill fly in all directions. Bears
love eating ants! But he was
a disappointed bear, because the
ant-hill had been deserted long
ago. And so, grumbling, he made
his way across to a wild plum tree.
Shinning rapidly up the smooth
trunk, he was soon perched in the
upper branches. It was only then
that he saw Chottu.

The bear at once scrambled
several feet higher up the tree and

laid himself out flat on a branch. It wasn't a very thick branch and left a large expanse of bear showing on either side. He tucked his head away behind another branch and, so long as he could not see the boy, seemed quite satisfied that he was well hidden, though he couldn't help grumbling with anxiety. Like most animals, he could smell humans, and he was afraid of them.

Bears, however, are also very curious. And slowly, inch by inch, the young bear's black snout appeared over the edge of the branch. Immediately he saw Chottu, he drew back with a jerk and his head was once more hidden.

16

The bear did this two or three times, and Chottu, now greatly amused, waited until it wasn't looking, then moved some way down the tree. When the bear looked up again and saw that the boy was missing, he was so pleased with himself that he stretched right across to the next branch, to get at a plum. Chottu chose this moment to burst into laughter.

The startled bear tumbled out of the tree, dropped through the branches and landed with a thud in a heap of dry leaves.

And then several things happened at almost the same time.

The mother bear came charging

into the clearing. Spotting Chottu in the tree, she reared up on her hind legs, grunting fiercely.

It was Chottu's turn to be startled. There are few animals more dangerous than a rampaging mother bear, and the boy knew that one blow from her clawed forepaws could finish him.

But before the bear reached the tree, there was a tremendous roar, and the tiger bounded into the clearing. The bears turned and ran, the younger one squealing with fright. The tiger had been asleep nearby and the noise had woken him, putting him in a very bad mood.

He looked up at the trembling
boy, and roared again.

Chottu nearly fell out of the tree.
"Good-day to you, Uncle," he

stammered, grinning nervously.

With a low growl, the tiger turned his back on Chottu and walked away, his tail twitching with annoyance.

Chapter 3

But then something happened which changed the hunting habits of the tiger and brought him into conflict with the villagers.

There had been no rain for almost two months, and the tall grass had become a sea of billowy dry yellow. Some city-dwellers, camping near the forest, had been careless while cooking and had

started a forest fire. Slowly it
spread into the interior of the forest,
and drove the tiger out towards the
edge. As night came on, the flames
grew more vivid, the smell stronger.
The tiger turned and made for the
marsh, where he knew he would be
safe provided he swam across to
the little island in the centre.

The next day he was on the
island, which was untouched by the
fire. But his surroundings had

changed. The slopes of the hills were black with burnt grass, and most of the tall bamboo had disappeared. The deer and the wild pig, finding that their natural cover had gone, had moved further east.

For the next four days the tiger hunted through the forest but found no food. By now he was so hungry that he even resorted to rooting among the dead leaves and burnt out stumps of trees, searching for worms and beetles.

But he hesitated to leave the area in search of new hunting grounds, for he had a deep fear of the unknown forests further east. He could have gone north, into the high mountains, but they did not provide him with the long grass he needed for cover.

Early one morning he came to the marsh. The water was now shallow and muddy, and a green scum had spread over the top. He drank, and then lay down across his favourite rock, hoping for a deer; but none came. He was about to get up and lope away when he heard an animal approach.

The tiger at once slipped off his rock and flattened himself on the ground.

A buffalo emerged from the forest and came to the water.

The buffalo was alone.

He was a big male, and his long curved horns lay right back across his shoulders. He moved leisurely towards the water, completely unaware of the tiger's presence.

The tiger hesitated before making his charge.

It was a long time – many years – since he had killed a buffalo, and he knew that the villagers would be angry. But the pangs of hunger overcame his caution. There was no morning breeze, everything was still, and the smell of the tiger did not reach the buffalo.

Crawling stealthily on his stomach, the tiger skirted the edge of the marsh and approached the buffalo from behind. The buffalo was standing in shallow water, drinking, when the tiger charged from the side and sank his teeth into his victim's thigh.

The buffalo staggered, but turned to fight. He snorted and lowered his horns at the tiger.

But the big cat was too fast for the brave buffalo. He bit into the other leg and the buffalo crashed to the ground. Then the tiger moved in for the kill.

After resting, he began to eat. Although he had been starving for days, he could not finish the huge carcass. And so he dragged the remains into the bushes, to conceal it from jackals and vultures; then he went off to find a place to sleep.

He would return when he was hungry.

Chapter 4

The herdsmen were naturally very upset when they discovered that a buffalo was missing.

And next day, when Nandu and Chottu came running home to say that they had found the half-eaten carcass near the marsh, the people of the village grew angry. They knew that once the tiger saw how easy it was to kill their animals, he would do so again.

Kundan Singh, Nandu's father, who owned the buffalo, said he would go after the tiger himself.

"It's too late now," said his wife. "You should never have let the buffalo roam on its own."

"He had been on his own before. This is the first time the tiger has attacked one of our animals."

"He must have been hungry," said Chottu.

"Well, we are hungry too," said Kundan. "It was our best buffalo – the only male in the herd. It will cost me at least two thousand rupees to buy another."

"The tiger will kill again," said

Chottu's father. "Many years ago there was a tiger who did the same thing. He became a cattle-killer."

"We will have to shoot the tiger tonight, when he returns to the carcass for another meal," said Kundan.

That evening, accompanied by Chottu's father and several others, Kundan set out for the marsh, where, without shifting the buffalo's carcass – for they knew the tiger would not come near them if he suspected a trap – they made a tree-platform in the branches of a tall tree some ten metres from the kill.

Then, Kundan and Chottu's

father settled down for the night on their rough platform.

Several hours passed and nothing but a jackal was seen by the watchers. Suddenly the two men were startled by a low "A-oonh".

Kundan tightened his grip on the gun. There was complete silence for a minute or two, then the sound of stealthy footfalls on the dead leaves beneath the tree.

A moment later the tiger walked out into the moonlight and stood over his kill. At first Kundan could do nothing. He was completely taken aback by the size of the tiger. Chottu's father had to nudge him, and then Kundan quickly put the gun to his shoulder, aimed at the tiger's head, and pressed the trigger.

The gun went off with a flash and two loud bangs. There was a tremendous roar. The tiger rushed at the tree and tried to leap into the

branches. Fortunately, the platform had been built at a good height, and the tiger was unable to reach it.

He roared again and then bounded off into the forest.

"What a tiger!" exclaimed Kundan, half in fear and half in admiration.

"You missed him completely," said Chottu's father.

"I did not," said Kundan. "You heard him roar! Would he have been so angry if he had not been hit?"

"Well, if you have only wounded him, he will turn into a man-eater – and where will that leave us?"

"He won't be back," said Kundan. "He will leave this area."

During the next few days the tiger lay low. He did not go near the marsh except when it was very dark and he was very thirsty. The villagers decided that the tiger had gone away. Nandu and Chottu – usually accompanied by other village boys, and always carrying their small hand-axes – began bringing the buffaloes to the marsh again during the day; they were careful not to let any of them stray far from the herd.

But one day, while the boys were taking the herd home, one of the buffaloes lagged behind.

Nandu did not realize that an animal was missing until he heard

an agonized bellow behind him.
He glanced over his shoulder just
in time to see the tiger dragging the
buffalo into a clump of bamboo.
The herd sensed the danger, and
the buffaloes snorted with fear as
they hurried along the forest path.
To urge them forward and to
warn his friends, Nandu cupped his
hands to his mouth and gave a
yodelling call.

The buffaloes bellowed, the
boys shouted, and the birds flew
shrieking from the trees. Together
they stampeded out of the forest.
The villagers heard the thunder of
hoofs, and saw the herd coming
home amidst clouds of dust.

"The tiger!" called Nandu. "He is back! He has taken another buffalo!"

He is afraid of us no longer, thought Chottu. And now everyone will hate him and do their best to kill him.

"Did you see where he went?" asked Kundan, hurrying up to them.

"I remember the place," said Nandu.

"Then there is no time to lose," said Kundan. "I will take my gun and a few men, and wait near the bridge. The rest of you must beat the jungle from this side and drive the tiger towards me. He will not escape this time, unless he swims the river!"

Chapter 5

Kundan took his men and headed
for the bridge across the river, while
the others, guided by Nandu and
Chottu, went to the spot where the
tiger had seized the buffalo.

The tiger was still eating when
he heard the men coming. With an
angry grunt he bounded into the
forest, and watched the men through
a screen of leaves and tall grass.

They carried hand drums slung from their shoulders, and some carried sticks and spears. After a hurried consultation, the men strung out in a line and entered the forest beating their drums.

The tiger did not like the noise. He went deeper into the forest. But the men came after him, banging away on their drums and shouting at the tops of their voices. He could easily have broken through the line of men – but, more than anything, he wanted to get away from the noise.

The tiger was not a man-eater and he would not attack a man unless he was very angry or very frightened; and as yet he was neither. He had eaten well, and he would have liked to rest – but there would be no rest for him until the men ceased their tremendous clatter.

Nandu and Chottu kept close to their elders, knowing it wouldn't be safe to go back on their own. Chottu felt sorry for the tiger; he hadn't forgotten the day when the tiger had saved him from the bear.

"Do they have to kill the tiger?" he asked.

"If they drive him across the river he won't come back, will he?"

"Who knows?" said Nandu. "He has found it's easy to kill our buffaloes, and when he's hungry he'll come again. We have to live too."

Chottu was silent. He could see no way out for the tiger.

For an hour the villagers beat the forest, shouting, drumming, and trampling the undergrowth.

The tiger had no rest. Whenever he was able to put some distance between himself and the men, he would sink down in some shady spot to rest; but, within a few minutes, the trampling and drumming would come nearer, and with an angry snarl he would get up again and pad northwards, along the narrowing strip of forest, towards the bridge across the river.

It was about noon when the tiger finally came into the open. The boys had a clear view of him as he moved slowly along. He was still out of range of Kundan's gun, but he was trapped.

He disappeared among some bushes but soon reappeared to retrace his steps. The beaters had done their work well. The tiger was now only about one hundred metres from the place where Kundan waited.

Chottu, watching from a distance, wondered: Has he slipped through the beaters? And in his heart he hoped so.

Tins clashed, drums beat, and some of the men poked into the reeds along the river bank with their spears

or bamboo sticks. Perhaps one of
these thrusts found its mark, because
at last the tiger was roused, and with
an angry, desperate snarl he charged
out of the reeds, splashing his way
through an inlet of mud and water.

Kundan fired and missed.

The tiger rushed forward, making
straight for the bridge across the
river, which provided a route into

the hills beyond.

As he lurched across it, Kundan fired again, and this time the bullet grazed the tiger's shoulder.

The tiger bounded forward, lost his footing on the unfamiliar, slippery planks of the bridge, and went over the side, falling headlong into the swirling water of the river.

He rose to the surface once, but the current took him under and away, and before long he was lost to view.

Chapter 6

The boys lay flat on their backs on their little mud island, and watched the monsoon clouds gathering above.

"The king of the forest is dead," said Nandu. "That is the end of tigers."

"There have to be tigers," said Chottu. "Can there be an India without tigers?"

★   ★   ★

The river had carried the tiger many kilometres away from his old home and brought him ashore on the far side of the river, on a strip of warm yellow sand. Here he lay in the sun, quite still, breathing slowly.

Vultures gathered and waited at a distance, some of them perching on the branches of nearby trees. But the tiger was more drowned than hurt, and as the river water oozed out of his mouth, and the warm sun made new life throb through his body, he stirred and stretched, and his glazed eyes came into focus. Raising his head, he saw trees and tall grass.

Slowly he heaved himself off the ground and moved at a crouch to where the tall grass waved in the afternoon breeze. Would he be hunted again, and shot at? There was no smell of man. The tiger moved forward with greater confidence.

There was, however, another
smell in the air, a smell that reached
back to the time when he was
young and fresh and full of vigour;
something that he had almost
forgotten – the smell of a tigress.

He lifted his head and gave a
deep roar, "A-oonh!" And a roar
came back to him, calling him,
a roar that meant there would be
more tigers in the land!

That night, half asleep in his
bed, Chottu heard tigers roaring to
each other in the distance, and
he recognized the sound of his own
tiger. Then he knew that it was
alive and safe and he was glad.

50

"Good night, Uncle," he whispered into the darkness. "Let there be tigers forever."

THE EYES OF THE EAGLE

Chapter 1

It was a high, piercing sound, almost like the yelping of a dog.

Jai stopped picking the wild strawberries that grew in the grass around him, and looked up at the sky. He had a dog – a shaggy guard-dog called Motu (Hefty) – but Motu did not yelp, he growled and barked. The strange sound came from the sky, and Jai had heard it before. Now, realizing what it was, he jumped to his feet, calling to his dog, calling his sheep to start for home. Motu came bounding towards him, ready for a game.

"No, not now, Motu!" said Jai. "We must get the lambs home quickly." And again he looked up at the sky.

He saw it now, a black speck against the sun, growing larger as it circled the mountain, coming lower every moment; a golden eagle, king of the skies over the higher Himalayas, ready now to swoop and seize its prey.

Had it seen a pheasant or a pine-marten? Or was it after one of the

lambs? Jai had never lost a lamb to an eagle, but recently some of the other shepherds had been talking about a golden eagle that had been preying on their flocks.

The sheep had wandered some way down the side of the mountain, and Jai ran after them to make sure that none of the lambs had gone off on its own.

Motu ran about, barking furiously. He wasn't very good at keeping the sheep together – in fact, he was often bumping into them and sending them tumbling down the slope, but his size and bear-like appearance kept the leopards and wolves at a distance.

Jai was counting the lambs; they were bleating loudly and staying close to their mothers. One – two – three – four...

There should have been a fifth. Jai couldn't see it on the slope below him. He looked up towards a rocky ledge near the steep path to the Tung temple. The golden eagle was circling the rocks.

Suddenly the great bird stopped circling. It dropped a few feet, and then, wings held back and powerful feet thrust out below like the wheels of a plane about to land, it came swooping down, heading straight for a spot behind the rocks.

The bird disappeared from sight

for a moment, then rose again with a small creature grasped firmly in its terrible talons.

"It has taken a lamb!" shouted Jai. He started scrambling up the slope. Motu ran ahead of him, barking furiously at the big bird as it glided away over the tops of the stunted junipers to its eyrie on the cliffs above Tung.

There was nothing that Jai and Motu could do except stare helplessly and angrily at the disappearing eagle. The lamb had died the instant it had been struck. The rest of the flock seemed unaware of what had happened. They still grazed on the thick sweet grass of the mountain slopes.

59

"We had better drive them home, Motu," said Jai, and at a nod from the boy, the big dog bounded down the slope, to take part in his favourite game of driving the sheep homewards. Soon he had them running all over the place, and Jai had to dash about trying to keep them together. Finally they straggled homewards.

"A fine lamb gone," said Jai to himself. "I wonder what Grandfather will say."

Chapter 2

Grandfather said, "Never mind. It had to happen some day. That eagle has been watching the sheep for some time."

Grandmother, more practical, said, "We could have sold the lamb for three hundred rupees. You'll have to be more careful in future, Jai. Don't fall asleep on the hillside, and don't read storybooks when you are supposed to be watching the sheep!"

"I wasn't reading this morning," said Jai truthfully, forgetting to mention that he had been gathering strawberries.

"It's good for him to read," said Grandfather, who had never had the luck to go to school. In his days, there weren't any schools in the mountains. Now there was one in every village.

"Time enough to read at night," said Grandmother, who did not think much of the little one-room school down at Maku, their home village.

"Well, these are the October

holidays," said Grandfather, "otherwise he would not be here to help us with the sheep. It will snow by the end of the month, and then we will move with the flock. You will have more time for reading then, Jai."

At Maku, which was down in the warmer valley, Jai's parents tilled a few narrow terraces on which they grew barley, millet and potatoes. The old people brought their sheep up to the Tung meadows to graze during the summer months. They stayed in a small stone hut just off the path which pilgrims took to the ancient temple. At 4,000 metres above sea level, it was the highest

Hindu temple on the inner
Himalayan ranges.

The following day Jai and Motu
were very careful. They did not let
the sheep out of sight even for a
minute. Nor did they catch sight of
the golden eagle.

"What if it attacks again?"
wondered Jai. "How will I stop it?"

The great eagle, with its powerful beak and talons, was more than a match for boy or dog. Its hindclaw, four inches round the curve, was its most dangerous weapon. When it spread its wings, the distance from tip to tip was more than two metres.

The eagle did not come that day because it had fed well and was now resting in its eyrie. Old bones, which had belonged to pheasants, snow-cocks, pine-martens and even foxes, were scattered about the rocks which formed the eagle's home. The eagle had a mate, but it was not the breeding season and she was away on a scouting expedition of her own.

The golden eagle stood on its rocky ledge, staring majestically across the valley. Its hard, unblinking eyes missed nothing. Those strange orange-yellow eyes could spot a field-rat or a mouse-hare more than a hundred yards below.

There were other eagles on the mountain, but usually they kept to their own territory. And only the bolder ones went for lambs, because the flocks were always protected by men and dogs.

Chapter 3

The eagle took off from its eyrie and glided gracefully, powerfully over the valley, circling the Tung mountain.

Below lay the old temple, built from slabs of grey granite. A line of pilgrims snaked up the steep, narrow path. On the meadows below the peak, the sheep grazed peacefully, unaware of the presence of the eagle. The great bird's shadow slid over the sunlit slopes.

The eagle saw the boy and the dog, but he did not fear them. He had his eye on a lamb that was frisking about on the grass, a few feet away from the other sheep.

Jai did not see the eagle until it swept round an outcrop of rocks about a hundred feet away.
It moved silently, without any movement of its wings, for it had already built up the momentum for its dive. Now it came straight at the lamb.

Motu saw the bird in time. With a low growl he dashed forward and reached the side of the lamb at almost the same instant that the eagle swept in.

There was a terrific collision. Feathers flew. The eagle screamed with rage. The lamb tumbled down the slope, and Motu howled in pain as the huge beak struck him high on the leg.

The big bird, a little stunned by the clash, flew off rather unsteadily, with a mighty beating of its wings.

Motu had saved the lamb. It was frightened, but unhurt. Bleating loudly, it joined the other sheep, who took up the bleating. It sounded as though they had all started complaining at once about the awful state of affairs.

Jai ran up to Motu, who lay whimpering on the ground. There was a deep gash in the dog's thigh, and blood was seeping onto the grass.

Jai looked around. There was no sign of the eagle. Quickly he removed his shirt and vest; then he wrapped his vest round the dog's wound, tying it in position with his belt.

Motu could not get up, and he was much too heavy for Jai to carry. Jai did not want to leave his dog alone, in case the eagle returned to the attack.

He stood up, cupped his hands to his mouth, and began calling for his grandfather.

"Dada, Dada!" he shouted, and presently Grandfather heard him and came stumbling down the slope. He was followed by another shepherd, and together they lifted Motu and carried him home.

Chapter 4

Motu had a bad wound, but Grandmother cleaned it and applied a
paste made of herbs. Then she laid
strips of carrot over the wound –
an old mountain remedy – and
bandaged the leg. But it would be
some time before Motu could
run about again. By then it would
probably be snowing and time to
leave these high-altitude pastures

and return to the valley.

Meanwhile, the sheep had to be taken out to graze, and Grandfather decided to accompany Jai for the remaining period.

They did not see the golden eagle for two or three days, and, when they did, it was flying over the next range. Perhaps it had found some other source of food, or even another flock of sheep.

"Are you afraid of the eagle?" asked Grandfather.

"I wasn't before," said Jai. "Not until it hurt Motu. I did not know it could be so dangerous. But Motu hurt it too. He banged straight into it!"

76

"Perhaps it won't bother us again," said Grandfather thoughtfully. "A bird's wing is easily injured – even an eagle's."

Jai wasn't so sure. He had seen it strike twice, and he knew that it was not afraid of anyone. Only when it learnt to fear his presence would it keep away from the flock.

The next day Grandfather did not feel well; he was feverish and kept in his bed. Motu was hobbling about on three legs; the wounded leg was still very sore.

"Don't go too far with the sheep," said Grandmother. "Let them graze near the house."

"But there's hardly any grass here," said Jai.

"I don't want you wandering off while that eagle is still around."

"Give him my stick," said Grandfather from his bed.

It was an old stick, made of wild cherry-wood, which Grandfather often carried around. The wood was strong and well-seasoned; the stick was stout and long. It reached up to Jai's shoulders.

"Don't lose it," said Grandfather. "It was given to me many years ago by a wandering scholar who

came to the Tung temple. I was
going to give it to you when you
got bigger, but perhaps this is
the right time for you to have it.
If the eagle comes near you,
swing the stick around your head.
That should frighten it off!"

Chapter 5

Clouds had gathered over the mountains, and a heavy mist hid the Tung temple. With the approach of winter, the flow of pilgrims had been reduced to a trickle. The shepherds had started leaving the lush meadows and returning to their villages at lower altitudes. Very soon the bears and the leopards and the golden

81

eagles would have the range all to themselves.

Jai used the cherry-wood stick to prod the sheep along the path until they reached the steep meadows. The stick would have to be a substitute for Motu. And they seemed to respond to it more readily than they did to Motu's mad charges.

Because of the sudden cold and the prospect of snow, Grandmother had made Jai wear a rough woollen jacket and a pair of high boots bought from a Tibetan trader. He wasn't used to the boots – he wore sandals at other times – and had some difficulty in climbing quickly up and down the hillside. It was tiring work trying to keep the flock together. The cawing of some crows warned Jai that the eagle might be around, but the mist prevented him from seeing very far.

After some time the mist lifted and Jai was able to see the temple and the snow-peaks towering behind it. He saw the golden eagle, too. It was circling high overhead. Jai kept close to the flock, one eye on the eagle, one eye on the restless sheep.

Then the great bird stooped and flew lower. It circled the temple and then pretended to go away. Jai felt sure it would be back. And a few minutes later it reappeared from the other side of the mountain, and it was much lower now, wings spread out and back, taloned feet to the fore, piercing eyes fixed on its target, a small lamb that had suddenly gone frisking down the grassy slope, away from Jai and the flock.

Now it flew lower still, only a few feet off the ground, paying no attention to the boy.

It passed Jai with a great rush of air, and as it did so the boy struck out with his stick and caught the bird a glancing blow.

The eagle missed its prey, and the lamb skipped away.

To Jai's amazement, the bird did not fly off. Instead it landed on the hillside and glared at the boy, as a king would glare at a humble subject who had dared to pelt him with a pebble.

The golden eagle stood almost as tall as Jai. Its wings were still outspread. Its fierce eyes seemed to be looking through and through the boy.

Jai's first instinct was to turn and

run. But the cherry-wood stick was still in his hands, and he felt sure there was power in the stick. He saw that the eagle was about to launch itself again at the lamb. Instead of running away, he ran forward, the stick raised above his head.

The eagle rose a few feet off the ground and struck out with its huge claws.

Luckily for Jai, his heavy jacket took the force of the blow. A talon ripped through the sleeve, and the sleeve fell away. At the same time the stick caught the eagle across its open wing. The bird gave a shrill cry of pain and fury. Then it turned and flapped heavily away, flying unsteadily because of its injured wing.

Jai still clutched the stick, because he expected the bird to return; he did not even glance at his torn jacket. But the golden eagle had alighted on a distant rock and was in no hurry to return to the attack.

Chapter 6

Jai began driving the sheep home.
The clouds had become heavy
and black, and presently the first
snowflakes began to fall.

Jai saw a hare go lolloping down
the hill. When it was about fifty
yards away, there was a rush of air
from the eagle's beating wings,
and Jai saw the bird approaching
the hare in a side-long dive.

So it hasn't been badly hurt, thought Jai, feeling a little relieved, for he could not help admiring the great bird. And now it has found something else to chase.

The hare saw the eagle and dodged about, making for a clump of junipers. Jai did not know if it was caught or not, because the snow and sleet had increased and both bird and hare were lost in the gathering snow-storm.

The sheep were bleating behind him. One of the lambs looked tired, and he stooped to pick it up. As he did so, he heard a thin whining sound. It grew louder by the second. Before he could look up, a huge wing caught him across the shoulders and sent him sprawling. The lamb tumbled down the slope with him, into a thorny bilberry bush.

The bush saved them. Jai saw the eagle coming in again, flying low. It was another eagle! One had been vanquished, and now here was another, just as big and fearless, probably the mate of the first eagle.

Jai had lost his stick and there was no way in which he could fight the second eagle. So he crept further into the bush, holding the lamb beneath him. At the same time he began shouting at the top of his voice – both to scare the bird away and to summon help.

The eagle could not get at them now; but the rest of the flock was exposed on the hillside. Surely the eagle would make for them.

Even as the bird circled and came back in another dive, Jai heard fierce barking. The eagle immediately swung away and rose skywards.

The barking came from Motu. Hearing Jai's shouts and sensing

that something was wrong, he
had come limping out of the house,
ready to do battle. Behind him
came another shepherd and – most
wonderful of all – Grandmother
herself, banging two frying-pans
together.

The barking, the banging and the shouting frightened the eagles away. The sheep scattered, too, and it was some time before they could all be rounded up. By then it was snowing heavily.

"Tomorrow we must all go down to Maku," said the shepherd.

"Yes, it's time we went," said Grandmother. "You can read your storybooks again, Jai."

"I'll have my own story to tell," said Jai.

When they reached the hut and Jai saw Grandfather, he said, "Oh, I've forgotten your stick!"

But Motu had picked it up. Carrying it between his teeth, he brought it home and sat down with it in the open doorway. He had decided the cherry-wood was good for his teeth and would have chewed it all up if Grandmother hadn't taken it from him.

"Never mind," said Grandfather, sitting up on his cot. "It isn't the stick that matters. It's the person who holds it."